Son of the South

SON OF THE SOUTH

MARK STILL

Eusebius
PUBLISHING

With love for
my wife, Peggy, and daughter, Christie

Son of the South

Copyright © 1999, Mark Still

ISBN: 0-9669789-0-0

Cover illustration: Mark Still

Published by Eusebius Publishing

Eusebius Publishing Company
4744 Live Oak Canyon Rd.
La Verne, CA 91750
(909) 596-4778
EusebiusMS@hotmail.com

Printed in Canada

Acknowledgements

Special thanks to:

Professor Kathy Brindell, Chaffey College, Rancho Cucamonga, Ca.

Professor Barbara Mitchell, Chaffey College, Rancho Cucamonga, Ca.

Mike Simms – former curator, Camp Moore Conservancy, Tangipahoa, La.

Kathy Tarver, Port Hudson SCA, Zachary La.

Greg Potts, Port Hudson SCA Zachary La.

Mr. and Mrs. Boyd Penton, Watson, La.

Staff of Hill Memorial Library, LSU Baton Rouge, La.

Miller Dial and Lonnie Sibley, Camp Moore Museum and Park, Tangipahoa, La.

Louisiana Parishes in 1861

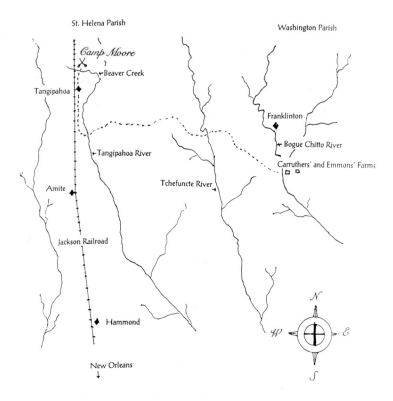

St. Helena Parish

Washington Parish

Camp Moore

Beaver Creek

Tangipahoa

Franklinton

Tangipahoa River

Bogue Chitto River

Carruthers' and Emmons' Farms

Tchefuncte River

Amite

Jackson Railroad

Hammond

New Orleans

N

W   E

S

Preface

*"There's many a boy here today who looks on war as
all glory, but, boys, it is all hell."*

This revealing statement, made by Union General
William Tecumseh Sherman in 1880, was his descrip-
tion of the war he knew – the American Civil War. Each
generation of Americans since that time has had to dis-
cover anew the seemingly obvious truth in that statement. The Civil War was the first "total war" in which
the battles involved civilians and cities, as well as the
military antagonists. It was also the first "modern war,"
ushering in a new era of warfare. Changes in the arts of
strategy and combat tactics were made necessary by the
development of new technologies, such as the machine
gun and the use of trenches and field fortifications. The
Civil War saw the first use of iron-clad ships and naval
"torpedoes," the military draft, mobile siege artillery,
and the use of railroads as a means of military trans-
port. It also saw the first terrifying beginnings of orga-

nized battlefield care for the wounded and dying. Extremely primitive by today's standards, the need for medical help in battle was often more horrific to the soldier than the warfare itself. There was no anesthetic before surgery or amputation, save an occasional shot of whiskey. There was no knowledge of infections and their causes. Of the estimated six hundred thousand combatants who perished in the Civil War, nearly two-thirds died of diseases and infections. Many who volunteered to serve their "country" never saw combat.

The Civil War was arguably one of America's greatest emotional experiences. It saw the tearing asunder of a nation over ideologies that were already outdated. It divided a nation over the preservation of its differences. It destroyed the South's economic way of life and the North's naivete of the costs of war. In dollars, it cost the United States government about $2 million dollars a day to prosecute the war, about eleven and one half billion dollars in post-war expenditures by the turn of the twentieth century. But the cost in homes, and families, and sons was incomprehensibly higher. The cost was so high that it caused President Abraham Lincoln to envision himself being drowned in the blood of American citizens.

In this essay, I have tried to impart a sampling of the thoughts, the feelings, and some of the experiences of war from the view of a common soldier through the vehicle of his letters to ones back home. The central figure of this essay, a young Louisiana boy, is a fictional composite of many real "sons of the South." I have endeavored to give a southern-sense to his writing, though, from specimens of the historic period, this character would have been more highly educated than the average teen of his time. This was necessary, to not only make the reading easier, but to more accurately portray the character's thoughts and passions to a contemporary audience. While the main character and his relations are fictional, the places, occurrences, battles, the officers and their units, are historic. I have drawn from many academic and archival sources to present a realistic account of the common human experience of a soldier who faces the enemy, and possibly death, on the battlefield.

Oliver Cromwell of England said in the mid-1600's, "When men run out of words, they reach for their swords." Most Americans who consider this statement might wish that it were otherwise. And yet, we consider words spoken by the Churchills, the Roosevelts, and the Lincolns, among our highest literary contributions when they proffer heroic confidence in time of war, even while the words of those persons who condemn war are rarely long remembered. In the final analysis, does war support the courageous "glories" that we envision? Is it, in the words of General George S. Patton, man's "greatest endeavor," one in which all other human endeavors shrink to insignificance? Or does war showcase the baseness and cruelty to which the highest order of life on the planet can sink, when we run out of words?

These are questions each generation has had to ask itself, since the practice of warfare began. As you read this essay, put yourself into the experience. Ask yourself the questions that have been considered since civilization began. Why do we make war? Is the practice of warfare justified by its results? If warfare is a natural instinct of our species, then what are the war's benefits to mankind? You will I am sure, find it easier to ask these questions of yourself during the reading of this essay than you would have on the battlefield.

Son of the South

July 9, 1861

Dear Mother Carruthers,

As you know by now, your son Thomas is dead. I regret at having lingered so long at writing you, but Col. Taylor has kept us moving since we left Camp Moore. Thomas and I got a lot of talking done before he died. I still can't imagine his not being here. I suspect I'll hear him calling to me just any minute, as he was always doing around the farm. "It was measles," the Doc said. There is a lot of dying here it seems, before we even get into this scrap. You know how powerful excited Thomas was to get into this fight. Back in April, Thomas came running down the road to my Pappy's farm to recite the news of the commencement of fighting. "Ford... Ford Emmons," he called. Thomas was running so hard I thought he was gonna slam hisself right into our gate. "Ford... git yourself up! Ol' Abe's gonna take on the South and git his comeuppance for sure!" You know how

Thomas has always been excitable, even when we was growing up together. Though my Daddy's old dogtrot cabin is down past the hill from yours, I thought Thomas and me was closer than most brothers. Anyway, I just thought you'd treasure knowing about Thomas' final days on this earth. I know he didn't write home much like you asked him to, but we was kept busy most of the time.

Thomas and me arrived at the training camp near Tangipahoa town next to the Jackson Railroad on June 26. It didn't hardly seem like we had gone very far since it was just about twenty miles from the farm. 'Course now, Thomas and me had never been past Franklinton before. You all probably don't know, but when Thomas and me was walking to school up to Franklinton all those days, we'd usually linger down to the Bogue Chitto and cut reeds or something. Thomas just couldn't keep hisself out of that old river, when the weather was warm. We was never getting to the old school house before Miss Mithener ringed the bell. Before long, I suspect she finally just gave up on us being timely.

As I was saying, when the officer signed us up, he asked Thomas if he was 18 yet. Well, you know Thomas didn't look all of his 16 years, to say nothing of 18. But Thomas just looked that officer straight in the eye and said, "I am over 18." Well... I have never heard Thomas lie in his life, to my recollecting! When we left the sign-up table, I said, "Thomas, I swear I have never heard you lay down a lie like that before in all our days." He said, "Ford, that was no lie! I wouldn't ever just tell a bold face lie to an officer, like that. But he was gonna keep me out of this fight. So when he asked if I was over

18, I allowed, as since my shoes are #18 and I was standing up, that I MUST be over them!" Well, we had a good laugh about that!

After we signed our names, we went to give our oaths as sons of Louisiana. As I recollect, it went close to the following; "You and each of you do solemnly swear true and faithful allegiance to the State of Louisiana, that you will defend her, that you will obey all orders in camp and will be subject to the orders of the Confederate States when formed into a regiment and having elected officers for the same, so help you God." Thomas' face looked like he had just become the King of Louisiana or something. I must be true and admit that I felt like I could lick the whole Union army by myself about then. The time has come though, when that kind of feeling is seeming awful ignorant. Colonel Taylor says that we are winning this here war, but I gotta admire some of them old Yanks. Some of those boys can really put up a scrap!

I'm supposing Thomas never told you about our regiment. We was formed into the 9th Louisiana regiment and Colonel Richard Taylor is in charge. Our Lt. Col. is E.G. Randolph, and the Major is W.J. Walker. I'm now in the Washington rifles bunch under 2nd Lt. Flut Magee. When me and Thomas first got here, we was saying that we was afraid the war would end before we could contribute. But old Flut says there's no fear of that.

We was mustered in this here army for twelve months. The time after getting here was spent cutting down trees to make room for our tents and getting settled in. Once the tents were up we spent most of each day learning to march and take orders. It comes more natural to some than others, that taking orders I mean. We was camped next to Major White's bunch from New Orleans. They are the noisiest bunch of levee rats that I ever did see. And they're so ready to fight they practice it every day amongst themselves. The Colonel put the whole camp under arms a couple times just to put down their rows. Those ol' boys would fight about anything. I thought, "One thing's for sure, if the rest of us Southern boys is like these here boys, we're bound to win this war or every man will perish in the effort." Well, we're not having to ante up like those Northern boys are doing just now, but I'm thinking our time will come.

They had Thomas and me detailed on picket duty after a couple days here in camp. We were detailed for 24 hour shifts, but then relieved every 2 hours. That means that we're on picket for two hours then we're off for four hours rest, then we go back and relieve the pickets again. It's like that for a day and a night then another bunch takes the duty. I know Thomas was not liking to be out there by hisself at night. Sometimes somebody would start shooting and we never knew if it was the Northern army or just some row near camp. Most of the complaining that I heard from Thomas though, was about the food. We'd get that plate of lean pork, some beans or rice, and an old hard biscuit, and Thomas would start recounting as how his Ma must be the best cook in the world. He'd go on about how you would git up some butter beans, or a stew, and make simple eating like a little slice of heaven. I'd allow as how he had better keep his mouth full of what he's got on his plate instead of making these here boys hungry for home, or there'd be the devil to pay for sure.

Well now, there's six fine boys to a tent, and all the tents lined up in neat rows right next to the woods. First thing, Thomas went about sweeping the dirt floor of our tent. He said he was "gonna rid us of the piney needles, acorns, and rocks." Well, you know as good as me that Thomas was afraid of waking up with some other creature sleeping next to him. I just let it be, but the other boys went out and gathered back some of those piney needles to put under their thin blankets to soften their beds. Once all these here boys got to sleep, I don't know if we would hear a Northern attack or not for all the snoring.

We spent four or five hours a day at drilling, then Thomas and me would go by the guardhouse to see if we knew anyone there. Sometimes we would go over to the sutler's shed and see if he had any provisions and such we might need, but we weren't sure just what our needs was gonna be. Besides the headquarters tent and the quartermasters and commissary tents, there was a booth of fancy stores and drinks. On occasion, Thomas and me and a few others would walk down to Beaver Creek on the south end of camp. Sometimes the water was too dirty to drink due to the camp's use, but it still felt cool to lay in after a day of drilling. Mostly, all of us were just bored and eager to get into this scrap.

On July second, we commenced to target training with our rifles. We was drilled in how to carry and take care of them. Since Thomas and me have always, as far back as I can recollect, had a rifle and could use them, I felt that they was wasting our time. None of these other boys here seemed to need the practice either. Once they gave us powder and shot, they had to notice what good shots we are. We took our mandatory four shots, but if we wanted to shoot anymore we had to use our own powder and shot, as most of the ammunition went to the boys that are fighting. I guess you know that Thomas brought his grandpa's powder horn with him from home. Thomas allowed that since Old Pap had carried it in the old fellow's war, it just might bring him good luck in this one. Thomas asked me before he died to carry it with me when I go up against the Yanks, so it's luck would now be mine. But I reckoned you would probably want it back, so I sent it home to you with Thomas' personals. The small package I sent home to you was all the property that Thomas' had here at camp. I kept a daguerreotype picture of the two of us that we had made in the camp. I keep a note with it telling whoever finds it, that if something happens to me, they are to send it to you. I trust that will be done.

Last night we heard that the officers telegraphed Jeff Davis a day or two ago, that our regiment is ready to march in defense of our homeland. Some of the boys want to get moving so as to begin counting off their twelve months of service. Please excuse my faltering pen as I am leaning against a beech tree with my paper on my thigh, and it is now beginning to rain again. Yes sir, we've got all the comforts of home!

Well, I said that Thomas and me got a lot of talking done before he died. Once his fever got up to serious high, the Doc had Thomas moved from our tent into the hospital tent. The Doc said that if any of his tent fellows was gonna git what Thomas had, it was better that they go ahead and git it in camp and not on the move to battle. I was allowed to visit Thomas whenever I wasn't drilling or on duty. There was about a dozen other boys in the hospital along with Thomas, and one of them died before Thomas did. Eddie Hart from Franklinton School is here. He's only fourteen years old. The majority of the boys here at Camp Moore seemed to be in their fourteenth, fifteenth, or sixteenth year. I'm sure their ages are known to the officers, but they seem to be willing to take just about anyone for this army. Sometimes one or more of the ladies from town come in and take letters from the sick men to post to their families, or help the Doc by wetting the fevered brow of some of these poor old boys. Their presence seemed to give the men a lifting in their spirits by their kindness. Especially when some boys left camp on the cars, I couldn't help but notice how everyone hereabouts was ready to lend a hand in kindness to their "fighting boys," or do whatever needed doing for their homeland.

When the Doc moved Thomas into the hospital tent I could tell he was really scared that he was gonna die. He said that, "nobody that goes into that tent comes out on his own power." His first day in the hospital was the hardest, I think. I know that Thomas was powerful lonely by hisself, but as his fever grew higher he spent most of his time sleeping. I spent all the time I could with him. Most of the time Thomas did not know who I was, due to delirium from fever.

When we could talk in the three days that he hung on, Thomas would remind me of something that we did when we was growing up, and always git the tale so twisted 'round you'd hardly recognize it. One day back when he was about ten years old, we walked down to that old broken bridge on the Bogue Chitto and sat a spell just looking into the water. Directly Thomas said, "What do you think it would be like to be a fish?" I said that I had never put my mind to thinking about it since there wasn't much likelihood that I was ever gonna need to know. After being quiet for a spell, Thomas said that he thought the worst part of being a fish was that they can only eat fish food. Well... with that, I just had to knock him off that bridge and into the water! Thomas said that it was he who threw me off the bridge, but I know better. I suppose boys do a lot of stupid things, growing up.

Thomas talked a lot about his grandpa's passing all those years ago. Ole Pap used to tell both of us stories about the war against the British. Thomas especially liked when Ole Pap told about how they fought like the Indians do, and how the British would always line up and march right into the settler's musket fire. According to Ole Pap, all the colonials used to do was stack up dead British soldiers like cord wood. I gotta admit, Old Pap could really tell an exciting tale. I think he forgot a whole lot about what the real fighting was like, though. Maybe he chose to forget. The real war is nothing to tell a couple of young pups like we were about. I hope I'll be able to forget someday when this is all over, but it won't be any time soon, that's for sure. I don't know how much of Old Pap's stories Thomas took as true, but I know that Thomas had a great respect for Old Pap, and the other old men who fought for our freedom. I think Thomas was anxious to do his part in this war, so his grand babies would look up to him, as he looked up to

Old Pap. I suppose nobody can give someone else a good accounting of what a war is really like, lest they was there as well. On Sunday, while I was talking to him, Thomas just closed his eyes and stopped breathing. I just sat there looking at him for a long time. I couldn't get it in my mind that he was gone. Thomas was laid to rest in the camp cemetery, just about a hundred yards from where our tent is set up. I'm gonna put down my pen for now because I have picket duty soon and I haven't eaten yet.

July 11th

I woke up this morning before light and thought I was back home for a time. I awoke with the smell of the dewy ground in my nostrils, just like when Thomas and me used to pass those summer nights out under old "spooky tree." I know you remember how, some warm evenings, we'd go up to that old oak on the hill between our farms and lay down in the grass and imagine all the scary things up in the tree by the moonlight. On about by morning, we could smell the dew on the grass, and hear the screech of the cicadas, as we dosed in and out of sleep. When we woke up with the light, everything always seemed so new and bright. There was nobody stirring yet at the houses, but we knew our chores were waiting so we'd head on down the hill with our bare feet smooshing in the wet grass. It's funny about those remembrances that come to you when all is quiet and peaceful. I feel powerful lonely with Thomas gone.

Last night, John Wadsworth gave me a taste from his tin of Gillet and Knevel sardines. He told me that they came all the way from France, across the Atlantic

Ocean. After a sample, I gotta say that the French are powerful in need of some good Southern cooking! I am thinking about them now again because they loaded us just like those sardines into the freight cars this morning to move us up to Virginia. I guess the boys have finally gotten their wish. We're off to do our duty against the Yankees. It's raining from time to time, as it has been for two days now. The wet sure raises a stinking perfume in these cars. We just can't tell if the smell is from the animals that used these cars before us, or from these poor old boys' soaking hides! One thing's sure, with all the rain we've been getting of late, the corn in my Papa's west plot should be near ready to cut. I reckon that all the southern corn crops will double this year due to the heavy wet season. I wish we could have planted more this last season so Papa could have sold some for cash. With me gone soldiering though, Papa will have a time getting the crops in by hisself.

The train just stopped at Grand Junction in Tennessee. We all piled out of the cars like a herd of hogs heading for the trough. This is my first time out of Louisiana, but I can't say that I'm too greatly impressed so far. We'll be heading out to Chattanooga as soon as the wood and water for the engine is loaded, and the engineers are fed. There is some talk of us soldiers eating in Chattanooga, but the officers aren't saying for sure. The worst part of the travel is that it is hard to ever sit down in the cars. Besides being cramped, the floor is wood and splintered by the animal stock that the cars are used to carrying. I'm going to try an open platform car if available when we reload. I don't suppose I can get much wetter anyhow.

I wrote Papa just before we headed out on the cars but haven't made the time since then. I would be pleased if you tell him, should you see him, that I am well and have no complaints. I saw his cousin Nathan before I left the camp. He said he'd been up near Clinton, at Hermon's Corners, and secured a newspaper. We get the war news by littles, except for passing travelers, and their news is not always quite factual. Nathan said he would head over to Papa's directly, and take news of me with him.

You know, Thomas was eager to ride the cars since he had never done so before. But if he's looking down right now, I hope he sees that the experience sure seems more a-cricket in our boots than a pleasurable trip. One of the boys in our car allowed that since we was all herded into these cars like cattle, he was a-wondering where the cows are riding. The older men allow as how even this kind of traveling beats walking. I don't know. A vote on it might surprise some folks, I think. Lt. Flut just told us that we will be fed in Chattanooga. I'm getting so hungry, I believe I could eat Wadsworth's last sardine. I'm sure you would not know me from when I left home, due to the fact that I've lost weight. The older men say I've just lost my baby fat. All I know is, I had to trade a pair of socks for some saddle-strap just to keep my pants up! Well, they did feed us at Chattanooga as they said they would. But it was nothing to right home about, so I won't.

July 21st

After we passed Knoxville, Tennessee, we headed toward Richmond, Virginia. The last night we passed on

21

the cars was more to my liking, as far as weather is concerned. There was still no room to sit down, but I leaned against the wall of the car and dozed on and off. There was a row in the car ahead of us last night. We all heard the ruckus. If Thomas had been here, he would of heard some of the finest cuss words of his life! I had to ask the older men what some of those words meant before I could rightly appreciate them, though. One of the older men said that we was gonna hear the highest cuss words when we faced the Yanks in battle. We arrived at Manassas Junction, near Richmond today, late in the afternoon. They told us at the station that there had been fighting round about here for the last four days. Chatham Wheat's Louisiana Tigers have been engaged with the Yanks most of the day. We were anxious to get into the scrap, but we were too late to take part. "The Yanks are on the run back to Washington City," they told us. We would have to get organized, and draw our rations and shot, before we would be ready to participate. So we commenced to getting lined up into our regiments and preparing to begin our part in this war in the morning.

July 22nd

Upon arising, came the news that C. R. Wheat, who I mentioned earlier, was badly wounded through the lungs in battle yesterday. It is not known if he will survive or not. The other news says that Jeff Davis visited General Beauregard's headquarters at Manassas Junction late last night. I missed my chance to see our new President by trying to catch up on my sleeping! Lt. Flut said that some of us boys could hike on up from the

Junction this morning and see the battlefield from yesterday's fight. I guess this is to be our first look at what war is all about. I am so excited, I can't even eat my breakfast.

There are soldiers detailed from both sides trying to remove the dead soldiers over to trenches for burial. The bodies are all swollen and some of their faces are split open and covered in flies. The smell is beginning to overcome some of us. I see others bent over a fence rail, or whatever is handy, puking up their breakfasts. I was just thinking, that all this while back at Camp Moore we were all talking about fighting, and how we were going to slaughter those Yanks. We never thought about what happened to those poor old boys that are left behind. I guess there aren't many of us that ever took part in this kind of fighting before. I heard many say that they've never seen bodies of such number, and in such condition before. Death seems like such a clean, quick business in our minds, but it isn't for sure. One poor old Yank didn't have a recognizable head anymore. Another who, by his face looked like he hadn't died very quickly, had most of his chest blown away. One of our Virginia boys had been shot three or four times, and his arm was laying about four feet from the rest of his body. A sergeant who was helping to remove the bodies told us to lend a hand, and gather up all the usable items from the dead. It seemed so sad to take a man's belt and packs, his shoes and socks, and whatever else that wasn't torn up, to give to another soldier. It made me think as how this poor old dead soldier doesn't seem worth as much as his equipment is. I couldn't help but wonder who this poor boy was. I hope there is someone back home who will mourn for him. There should be someone to mourn the passing of every man who dies on a battlefield, I think. From the faces of those helping out here, it looks like most of us are having second thoughts about our great "adventure". I don't want to kill someone's pa, or brother, or only son. I took up my country's call to just kill Yanks!

It seemed like a much longer hike back to camp, than coming out here. There wasn't much talking among the boys. One boy took a souvenir off some dead Yank back on the battlefield. It is some kind of locket with pictures in it of some lady, probably the poor man's wife. I told the boy that he should leave the pictures on the Yank so's they would be buried with him, 'cause it might give the man comfort. Instead, I think he just tore up the pictures and kept the locket. Back at camp, Flut told us that the weapons are picked up off the battlefield as soon as the battle is over, but it usually takes a few days to bury the dead. Sleeping won't come easy tonight, I think.

July 24th

I was surprised and pleased to receive your kind letter this morning. I wish you wouldn't think that Thomas died in vain. I know that he passed before he could get into the fight, but I feel sure that Thomas is tagging along right beside me now, as he always did. Anyway, I find myself thinking about him a lot. Sometimes I feel like I could just commence to talking to him, as if he was really right here with me. 'Course, it would scare the bejeebers out of me if he answered! I thank you for relaying news of me to Papa. I know that at times like these, he wishes that he had learned to write, but I know his feelings. I'm glad to hear that Ma Oakes and the others are also doing well. I was especially happy to hear that Uncle Cletus came to help Papa with the farming. With me gone soldiering, I know Papa needs the help. If I am true though, I would have to admit to you that I would have never thought that old Cletus would lend a hand to anybody in who's in need. Well, sometimes relations do surprise you.

Right now we are waiting around to find out what to do, and where to go next. Old Flut said that we will be receiving our orders directly. I never realized how much waiting that's involved in soldiering. Most of the men are complaining that, since we arrived too late yesterday to participate in the fighting, we should be hurrying off and after the invaders. They talk as if the war would now be over if only we had arrived in time to get our licks in. I'm thinking that, after seeing the battlefield this morning, I'm not so sure that Thomas and me didn't make a hasty decision in joining this fight. I suppose it is too late to worry over such things now, but I reckon I never really considered the prospect of being killed in this little fight. I'd be honest in saying that I'm sure considering it now.

July 25th

This morning Captain Richardson ordered us to arms and full packs. He marched us south about ten miles, but I can't say exactly where we're heading. I don't mean that it is some military secret or something, I really just don't know where we are or where we are headed. The ground is mostly tree covered. I know Papa

25

could make some real money with a stand of trees like these. All the good lumber has already been sold off our farm, as you know.

There was a downpour of rain along the way, but it only lasted about twenty minutes or so, just long enough to soak us to the skin. While we are here resting, one of the boys got out his mouth harp and is entertaining the troops on it. It's truly amazing how a body can find the energy to carry on to a good Southern tune, when just minutes before he thought he could not make another step. The Captain has ordered us to our feet, so I guess I'll write some more in another ten miles or so.

(Evening, the 25th)

We had marched about three miles more when we heard shots up ahead. Flut ordered us to form a line at an angle from the road, and find cover until the Captain could find out what was happening up ahead. While we was waiting, it started to rain again. The Captain ordered us to dig some trenches and pile the dirt up in front to give us protection, as we might be heading into a fight soon. We had to take special care to keep our powder dry, and our rifles out of the mud. Directly, the shooting ahead of us started up again, but this time it seemed closer. Then it stopped! Our advance skirmishers came a-running back to our lines, and we were told to wait for orders before we commence to firing. Except for the officers moving back and forth behind us, it seemed to be deathly quiet along our line. I have no recollecting of the time that passed while we waited there in the mud. None of us knew what to expect, or how we would react when the Yanks attacked. Some of the boys were praying. Some of us just laid there, barely breathing.

After some time, we thought we could hear the sound of horses coming up in the trees ahead. Then suddenly, we saw them! There were just two horses with boys dressed in gray on them. They were marching three Yanks in front of them that they had just captured. That's what the shooting in front of us was. As far as we could make out, these Yanks had run away from the battle the day before, but ran south smack into two of our boys on the road. There wasn't much talking among us in the next few miles, as everyone felt a little shameful at our thoughts and actions. Tonight we set up camp near a crossroads on our way to the river coast.

July 28th

I saw the famous Potomac River for the first time this morning. It is the widest river that I have ever seen. My company was sent to a landing place (I don't know the name) on the river to guard the unloading of some supplies. We was all interested in what was being unloaded, hoping for food supplies. We haven't had much to eat besides rancid meat and hard biscuits since we arrived on the cars. We was told, though, that the supplies was mostly military items and blankets and such.

Later in the day, we marched back up the same road we had just come down. We went back to the same cross roads and set up camp again for the night. So far this here war ain't much but hiking around the country side. I'm thinking that maybe we should dare the Yanks to a hiking contest and that would settle this fight. I'm sure we would win if they picked our company to test. Well, I guess all the spare time I have is good, or I wouldn't have time to write much. Two of the boys in our company was stricken down with the fever today. It seems to strike very suddenly and I find myself anxious as to whether I might be struck down. So far, I'm feeling strong, so don't you let my family go worrying none about it. It sure wouldn't hurt none of us, though, to have a plump chicken or some other fresh meat for supper on some of these days. The sergeant sent a few of the boys out to do some foraging in the local area. Maybe they will come back with a cow or a few hogs that we can render into a fitting dinner. I'm feeling like the worst part of this here army is the food. It wouldn't hurt us too much to find a good stream with enough water in it to take a bath. I haven't been out of these clothes even once over the last seven days. The old doctor that's with us says that it don't matter how bad we smell, as long as we wash once in a every month, so that the bugs don't have a home on us to make youn'uns. Lord, have mercy! Now ain't that a nice thought when we're all sitting around eating our supper.

August 15th

Happy to receive your letter of July 20th. I can always cherish words from home. There is nothing new here. We're all doing what we seem to do best – just sitting around waiting for what we do not know.

August 25th

This morning they've got us up and drilling again. Most of us boys don't see the need to keep on marching and drilling when we think that we're never gonna get into this scrap. One of the boys in our company said that the South is going to challenge them Yanks to a drill, that's why we are all the day marching. If it's true, we had better put more effort into it. After all, we don't have such pretty uniforms, like those Yanks. I think they just want to keep us busy. After supper, I made friends with a boy named Joey Miller. He joined our ranks a couple of days ago, and has not had a good time of it. He said that he is fourteen years old, but I have doubts. It sounds like he has been pining for home almost since he left it. He's from over near General Lee's birth home, not too far from here. He reminds me a little of Thomas, I think.

As Joey and me sat near the cook fire just talking, several other fellows strolled up and joined in our conversing. Joey said that he thought that all the men would laugh at his being so homesick and all, but no one laughed. Even the old men had a tear in their eye when someone talked about his sweetheart or his momma back home. I can't see how a Yank could have as deep a love for his country as good southern men do. That's what will see us through to victory, I believe. The thought of giving up our way of life and sacred land to invaders from the north is just hateful to men from the South. Well anyway, I wasn't meaning to get grave, but I must be true and admit that, sitting there with those good and brave men, I could see that every man was realizing that he was fighting for his wife or sweetheart and the land that he loved. Right then, I think every man listening was proud that he is here.

November 20th

Sorry to all that I have not written for a couple of months. The officers are trying to keep us busy so as to not miss home so much. We have received no news of the war for some weeks. If we are still fighting the invaders, I am not aware of it. I will write again before long. Give my love and regards to all, and have a happy Thanksgiving dinner for me. I will be recollecting past times at home during our feast of salt pork and rice.

December 12th

Heavy rains in camp for the last several days has put a gloom on all of us. Aside from the usual drilling and such, we spend most of our time foraging for scraps of food for our regiment. The farms here abouts are stripped pretty clean, and the farmers are as hungry as we are. Since the war has slowed considerable with the turn of the weather, many here in camp were hopeful of time to go home. The officers say that it is unlikely that any of us will be allowed to return home for Christmas, so please give my best wishes to all for my thoughts will be with you as always.

December 25th

We will forever remember this Christmas for those things that we were lacking, rather than those things received. Most of the boys just sat around and played cards or dice. Of course if battle were at hand, the men would discard such things to divert the anger of the Almighty. There was the sounds of the season last night, as some of the boys gathered at the hospital tent to sing choruses. I am sure that it brought great comfort to the many poor sick and injured men. A minister came by to read from the Bible and lessen our afflictions. As is common at home, he also read the Christmas story. I sorely miss all of you and wish that I could be with you. Forgive me for saying this, but I am most powerfully grieved by the thought that this is the first Christmas for all of us without Thomas. I do miss him so. This was his favorite time of the whole year.

January 1, 1862

I take pencil in hand to wish all back home a happy New Year. The minister was by to make a prayer for the success of liberty in the South, and for the soon end to the war. We are up to our knees in snow at this time. The army took over use of a farmhouse nearby to act as a hospital, as the tents won't stand up in the snow. In Christmas month alone, fifty-seven of our poor soldiers in camp died from diseases. Our grave yard is gitting crowded and the ground is too frozen to dig. The doctor just covers the dead in their blankets and stacks them to be covered by the snows. He says that they will have to wait until spring to be buried proper. Word just came by that we will have a weapons inspection in the morning to make sure that we are keeping our muskets battle-fit. Give my best to Papa, and to all the rest of the family.

March 3rd

I am pleased to receive your kind letter of February 15th, and grieved to hear of cousin Nathan's death. He always did git rowdy when he drank. I can not be too

31

surprised that it finally caught up with him. The weather has turned for the better, so our company spent the day beautifying the camp and clearing the brush. The country is nice, and everything is so pure and clean. Well, I am tired from today's enterprise, so I will seek my old friend wool Blanket and with many thanks, dream of home. My best to all.

April 4th

I am desperate to receive a letter from you, as I have not heard from home in near a month. There is not much new here, except that we have spent the month constructing the South's most beautiful, temporary camp. I have no doubt that we will surely move out soon, as our beautifying is now complete.

May 5th

Well, May has arrived and the weather gits warmer. All us in my tent were awakened this morning to a row at the north end of camp. It's been so dreadful boring with nothing happening in camp lately that we was excited to see something going on. Six fancy ladies arrived at camp this morning and the fellows was beside themselves to get a look at them. Major Walker was the first officer to make his way forward and he started warning us about diseases and such. I'm sure not one man in a dozen was paying him any mind. One of the older soldier boys explained to me that every army has its "followers," he called them. "They come along to keep the boys spirits up, and to remind us what we're fighting for," he said! "Where were they when the weather was cold and we needed their warmth?" I said.

Later in the afternoon, old buck-toothed Brian Jameson from Lt. Wadsworth's company, came around and said that spending time with the ladies cost as much as $20. I guess I'm just not very worldly, because it took me awhile to get the true meaning of all this. Major Walker said that more men in this army are dying from the diseases than from the enemy's bullets. With Thomas dying from measles like he did, I guess I decided that it seemed easier to duck a bullet than a disease. At least I can see someone who is shooting at me.

We did have some great fun in the evening, though. One of J.J. Slocomb's young boys accidently fired off his musket, and shot the hat off the man standing next to him! Those boys was all over each other, and about an acre of camp as well. I think that I've never before seen such an entertaining fight. They knocked down two tents in the scuffle, then one of them landed in a cook fire and knocked over the kettle. It must have lasted 20 or 30 minutes. The officers just turned their backs and let the boys go at it. The boy with the musket broke his arm on a rock, so I think everyone will be safe from being shot for a few weeks. It was a sight though, and something to chat about for the next few days, I'm sure.

I'm just two months shy of a whole year in this here army. Other than an occasional hike for foraging, none of us in the 9th Louisiana have seen any real war. We spent a cold, wet winter just far enough from Richmond to be miserable. When weather permitted, we had quite a few visitors to the camp. Mostly they were relations of the soldiers that came, and then an occasional high ranking officer to look us over. The food is bad as always, when we git it. The hospital tent is full of soldiers with sickness as always. The doc told us the other day that he can't wait for an honest to goodness bullet wound just to break the monotony. In the past ten months, our regiment has lost about 173 men to diseases, and yet we still haven't heard many shots fired in anger. From time to time, we git news of battles. There was even one back home by Bayle's Cross Roads just before the end of the year, you probably know of it more than me. Most of the men are beside themselves feeling that we're missing out on this so called war. I think that if we don't git some action soon most of these boys are going to strike off on their own and find themselves some mischief to git into.

May 20th

It's May 20th, as close as I can reckon, and we are about to strike our tents for a hike that we believe will get us finally into this little scrap. General Banks' Union army, we've been told, has invaded Virginia and we're going to stop him. There's a lot of excitement in camp this day!

May 23rd

It took us three days of marching to git here, but we're hopeful that we will make a difference in the fight. The captain told us that up ahead is Front Royal, Virginia. Somewhere here in the Shenandoah Valley, old Abe has sent about 40,000 union soldiers. I sure hope we don't bite off more than we can chew. The order has come down to check our powder, shot, and supplies. We're to make sure that we are ready in every way for immediate battle. As the officers line us up behind the trees, I admit to you that I am excited and also scared. I'm thinking back right now on that little fracas back in the woods of Virginia. We waited and waited for the enemy to get close enough to git them in our sights, and all the while we was shaking in our boots. Now, we don't know what is up ahead. Some of the boys is praying, some are calmly checking their rifles and shot, one young boy just retched up his breakfast. The waiting is the worst part of war. Last week I would have said that the boredom was the worst. But right now everyone is wondering if this is their last day in this world. I hear the order to git ready.

(Evening, the 23rd)

Well, they say that it was an easy victory. Most of our company made it back. About noon, General Jackson hisself gave the order to charge. As we came out of the trees, I could see the small settlement in front of us. The union had set up an outpost on the edge of town, and that was our first target. It seemed like forever between the trees and the town. I saw some men in the front of the line fall, and others moved up to take their place. As we started double-timing, most of the southern boys started screaming and hollering. It seemed to scare the bejeebers out of the Yanks. We just kept running and running. Soon we had run clean out of town, and our officers was yelling at us to reform. I felt good that we had won this fight, and taken back part of the South. The union soldiers ran off to the north, reforming somewhere south of Winchester. But inside, I wasn't feeling too good. I only fired my musket once, but I saw the bullet find its mark. As we walked back through the town, I couldn't help but stop to see who I had just shot. He looked to be in his twenties, and I was grateful that he was not wearing a wedding ring. I stood there just staring at him for some time, his chest covered with the blood I spilled. Then I threw up. Lt. Flut came up directly and pulled me back to our lines. He reminded me that this fight was of the Yanks choosing, not ours. "If they would just go home and leave us in peace, we would not have to shoot them,"he said. After we made our camp for the night, a lot of the men fell directly to sleep. I couldn't sleep all night. I just couldn't git that man's face out of my mind. One of the men in our tent asked me if I would rather that it be me laying back there instead of that dirty Yank. I don't know, it just don't seem right.

May 28th

They've got us hiking again this morning. We engaged the enemy at Middletown on the 24th, and near Winchester on the 25th. Everyone's excited because the word is that we're going to Richmond. Those like me that haven't been there, are looking forward to seeing one of the most famous cities in the country. They're really moving us hard today. They say that we won't stop tonight until sometime after dark. We are to up and move out again.

May 30th

We marched about 50 miles in the last two days and we are all dog-tired. We didn't git as far as Richmond, but stopped to dig in about four miles north of Harrisonburg. Tomorrow, we're expecting to have the whole

Union army come marching right into our sights. General Ewell came around at supper time and told us to git a good night's sleep because we will be causing some real mischief in the morning. That is one of the easiest orders that I've ever gotten. Tomorrow is my 19th birthday. I had hoped to hear from home.

June 1st

We were engaged near Strasburg today. It is gitting to be sundown, so the light is fading. This is the first chance I've had to write for two days. Yesterday morning, General Fremont's Union boys came at us from the north as expected. I haven't been too impressed with these northern boy's fighting abilities. Sometimes they seem to lack the spirit to win the day, not that I'm complaining. Of course, they're only fighting because they are ordered to. They're not fighting to protect their homes and families like we are. We easily stopped their first charge. It seemed as though they weren't really up to a good scrap. Then, suddenly, we saw more blue coats than I thought existed. Thousands of them came at us and overran our front line. It was a frightful sight. The Captain ordered us to retreat to the trees at our rear, but some of the men was afraid of gitting shot in the back as if they was running away. My line retreated back about fifty yards, then turned to lay down another volley. As I looked back, I saw that all of those boys that wouldn't retreat was dead. I just kept loading my musket and firing as fast as I could, not noticing if my shot found its mark. The Yanks got within about twenty yards of my line before we turned them back. I was grateful that we wasn't ordered to re-advance back to our original positions, but were ordered to fall back another hundred yards and dig in. I'm not sure how we stopped them. Maybe they didn't have the spirit that our boys had. It sure looked to me like they should have broken through our lines, but they didn't.

It wasn't long until they came at us again. It seemed ignorant for them to cover the same ground twice. Our best snipers could pick them off even earlier than before. We fired volley after volley into the Yank lines, but they kept coming. Finally, we heard shooting off to our right side, and the Captain ordered our line to pivot and engage. We ran about forty yards and saw some of our boys retreating toward us. We found what cover we could and waited for the enemy to charge toward us. When the firing started, the man next to me was hit down by a bullet. Those damned Yanks just kept coming at us, and we just kept laying them down . Six of the men in our line was shot down. It wasn't a pretty sight, but I didn't have much time to think on it. I was loading and firing as fast as I could. Old Jake from Ponchatoula fell dead on top of me just as Lt. Flut yelled for "bayonets!" I was in a trench and couldn't git the poor man off of me, let alone reach into my belt for my bayonet. It seemed like forever trying to git situated and to my feet for the attack that I thought would surely kill me too. Once I was up and ready, I couldn't see any Yanks within fighting distance, so I dropped back down into my trench and kept firing. Bullets was hitting the ground all around me and I could hear them whining past my ears, too. All that I could think was that any second one of those bullets was going to hit me. It had to! How could a body as big as me be missed with all these bullets flying around? I wondered if I was the only one left, and the whole Yank army was shooting at me! Suddenly, all the firing and yelling stopped. The Yanks was high-tailing it back to their cover, and our boys were trying to recover our lines. I took a deep breath, amazed that I was unhurt, and for the first time took a real look around me.

My Lord, there was bodies everywhere! The thin gray smoke from the artillery shot lifted from the soil into the air and gave the fields the look of hades. A man near me who earlier cried out that he was wounded, was now dead. I checked on Old Jake, but he was already gone. I will save you from a further true explanation of the scene, but there was more bodies than I could count – on both sides. I was ordered back to the supply wagon to bring up ammunition and hardtack for the men, but the battle was over for the day. The butchery around me was unbelievable. Three of the soldiers from my tent were dead. Everyone that I knew from my company, was dead. I just stood there and felt that, in some way, I was dead too... and so alone. Oh, how I want to go home.

Tonight, I'm thinking about Thomas again. With the fighting that we've had over the last couple of days, it's probably a direct act of God that I'm still alive. But, I feel sure that if Thomas had not died back at Camp Moore at the beginning of this mess, he surely would have died a much more painful and bloody death here in Virginia. I'm glad that he was spared the awful road that we've had to march. How ignorant we both was about war and all that goes with it. Our boys that was wounded in the battles of the last couple of days, though many will be going home now, have a hard life to look forward to. I'm imagining what life on Papa's farm would be like without the arms or legs to do the chores. What sweet southern girl would marry a man who couldn't even hold her in his arms? I pray that if I'm to be struck down in this fight, that I will quickly die rather than be crippled and have a hard, sad life. Mrs. Carruthers, I told my lieutenant that if something happens to me, he should contact you, as my Papa can't read. I hope you don't mind too much.

June 2nd

We just got word that about 6,000 southern boys lost their lives in the fighting here at Harrisonburg. They think that about as many Yanks died as well. But McClellan's army is still in Virginia, and trying to find a way to take Richmond. There is still the sound of musket fire in the distance from time-to-time. The word is that it is just skirmishers testing our lines. I'm very tired now, so I'll write more later.

June 5th

The weather is bad today, and even though it is raining, it is still hot. It's just like home! We're gitting ready for battle again, as the word is that the Yanks are expected to attack as soon as the weather lifts. We never know what to believe from the word in camp. It reminds me of Uncle Todd. I don't know if you've ever met Uncle Todd, but he is the one in our family who can spin some impressive yarns. Every family has one, I know. The problem is that before long even Uncle Todd doesn't remember what is the truth and what is the story. That's our case here in camp. It's best just to ignore all the talk and wait for orders.

June 7th

We're on the move again over to Port Republic, Virginia. The weather is sticky and hot, as usual lately. Last night the lieutenant told us we was having meat for supper, and everyone was really happy. It was maggot invested, and full of rot. Most of the boys ate it anyway figuring that once it was cooked, it made no matter. How do they expect us to fight if they don't feed us? One of the boys made some coffee out of chickory nuts. It seemed pretty tasty to us because none of us could remember what real coffee tastes like. A couple of boys from Jackson's regiment went out onto the battlefield and stripped the dead Union soldiers of all the food and supplies they was carrying before the burial details arrived. They said that the soldiers on both sides was using bent bayonets as body hooks to drag the dead boys into holes for burying. I lost the daguerreotype of Thomas and me that we got at Camp Moore. It causes me great distress because sometimes I can't remember his face very clearly, except in dreams of him which I have often. Please ask Papa again to send me some breeches and a shirt. All the clothes I have are in tatters, and I can't git replacements in the field. He can send them to Richmond, to my regiment, and I'll get them sooner or later. Will write more later. Love to all.

June 8th

This morning, we formed up our lines near the Shenandoah River. We got word that Fremont's Yanks was moving south again, so we had to block them. I couldn't see too far ahead of us, due to the trees. But we could hear the Yanks moving toward us. Our flankers came a'running back to our lines just after nine o'clock. They reported a large force of Yanks moving toward the grove of trees in front of us. Now the worst part – the waiting. About 9:30, a couple dozen Union calvary rushed our lines to test our defenses. Our sharpshooters cut them down before they was barely out of the trees. Then their infantry followed in behind them. Their first volley struck down a few of our boys, but we held the line. We gave them a volley, then retired to advance our second line. By this time, the bullets were flying thick and heavy. As usual, I just loaded and fired as fast as I could and hoped for the best result. Eventually, we drove the Yanks back into the trees. Our boys took 42 casualties, with 19 dead. We spent the rest of the day readying ourselves for their next attack. A couple of the boys became right agitated and asked the lieutenant to let them go off into the trees and pick off some of them Yanks. They said that it seems that we always wait to be attacked, rather than taking the occasion to do a little mischief of our own. The lieutenant said that he is under orders just like we are, and we will do what we're told to do. Well, that didn't sit well with the boys, but they fell into line anyway. By evening time, our company was called to take a rest position in the rear, which we did. We could hear occasional fighting going on and wondered how much rest we was going to get. Since the rains stopped, we have been beset with ticks and mosquitoes. They find us in our bedding when we sleep, and in our clothes when awake. When I'm called on to help clear the bodies from the battlefield, I'm always sickened by the bugs crawling in and out of eyes and noses and such. Well, I'm going to try to get some rest.

June 9th

This morning the fighting is heavier. Our company was assigned as rear guard for the day. I volunteered to carry supplies to the lines when needed. By noon, the fighting had shifted to Jackson's regiments, and our whole battalion was ordered to relocate to the east. There wasn't much action in our sector for the rest of the day, except some sniper shooting. The Yanks keep pecking away at our lines just to make sure we don't get any rest.

June 11th

Yesterday I received a slight wound on my neck. Please make sure that Papa don't get too excited about it. I rose up too far out of my trench and some quick Yank thought that he would bag a Reb. The old men say that I'm a real soldier now since I got shot. The doc fixed me up, then I went back to my company. Doc said that it is just like "stitching on a button." He is a terrible painful tailor. The worst part was the visit to the hospital tent. I didn't notice going in, but coming out I passed a cart full of arms and legs that the surgeons removed during the night. What a lamentable fate for these poor boys. The hospital area is the dirtiest area of the camp, it seems to me. I think I'd rather die then allow those surgeons to ply their trade on me.

I met a boy named Egan tonight. He was just in Richmond, and had some stories to favor the boys with.

He said that he had never been to a big city before and was really excited about going. But now he thinks that Richmond is like "one big stable." The smell of the horses was too great to imagine, he said. The manure was everywhere, and the horses trampled it into dust on the streets. Every breeze would deal it onto the clothes, the furniture, and into the noses of passers. He said, "I declare that I will never live in a big city with that constant horsey nosegay all about." Seems like the city people just pour their kitchen-slops out on the streets, along with the chamber dumps from the night before. All the men smell of beery breath, and little fatherless children run about everywhere. I think that I'd like to see that place though, if the chance presents itself.

A minister came by the camp last night, even though it wasn't Sunday. He preached about "surrendering all for Christ." He explained that what we are doing is fighting for God's own freedoms and rights, and that if we have to give up our own lives to keep our people and loved ones free, then God will stand next to us in our struggle. The preacher said that, even though many of us will fall in this great trial, we can rest assured that God will see to our ultimate victory because we are fighting for Him. I suppose that I never gave much heed to our little preacher back home. I never had much use for his Bible thumping, and speechifying. But I could tell that this preacher's words brought sincere peace to the boys in attendance. Now, as he said, we must all truthfully resolve whether we are ready and willing to give up our all for His cause. The preacher called on us to "buckle on the armor of Christian fortitude and ante up our pure sacrifice at the alter of love." I think to be truthful, I must admit that I'd rather the Yanks give up their all for the cause. Well, word has come down that we will be on the move again in the morning, so I'd better find something pleasant to pass the night dreaming about, and git to it.

June 14th

Last night we set up camp outside of Mechanicsville, to be in a better position to defend Richmond should the Yanks continue to push southeast. We have no word this morning of the Yanks movements, though. There are many sick boys in camp today. Six of them died yesterday of typhus fever. The lieutenant told us to stay with our own company today so as not to catch the sickness. But I need to see if I can trade something from my meager possessions for some socks or a shirt. Please remind Papa to send me some new breeches soon or I may have to take on the Yanks in nature's own way.

June 16th

With great pleasure I received your kind letter of May 3rd. I am sorry that all back home are so concerned over me. Please don't suffer yourself to despondency over my situation. I have determined to carry on as long as the infernal Yanks trouble our people. I regret to receive your news that Daniel Kibby was killed a few months ago. He was a good neighbor and soldier. I find that I would rather not git too close to any of the men anymore. It is so much harder when they git killed if you have spent time with them, even though it does git very lonely sometimes. A few of the men's wives are camping close by to be with their husbands as much as possible. Some of the wives freely give to other soldiers, as well. Their husbands know what is happening, but don't seem to fret over it. If the women were found fraternizing with a Yank though, I'm sure they would be killed outright for "harboring the enemy."

Mother Carruthers, I must ask a favor of you, though please do not tell Pa about it. If I should fall in battle, and my remains are located after the war, would you please make an effort to get me reburied back home with my family. Lately, the thought of spending eternity in foreign ground, even good Southern ground, away from Ma and my kin is more than I can carry. I know that what I'm asking is a great burden to you, so just say you will do this for me even if you know you won't. I've spent a year in this army and everyone that I've come to care about is dead. All together, we're just a bunch of southern boys who are all alone here. When I look into the eyes of the men in camp, it looks as though they are already dead but just still walking around. I have to suppose that I look the same to them. When someone takes out his banjo or mouth harp and commences to playing, there is no cheerful singing and clapping anymore. The songs about sweethearts and loved ones left back home now bring solemn stares and tears. Gone is the sweet pleasure that nestles itself in our bosoms in recollection of past times so precious. It's because we know now what death really is. It is not heroic, or courageous. It is not, like the poet said, the affirmation or vindication of right over wrong. It is just death! It is painful, and messy, and final, for both sides. It walks right beside us every day. Well, please forgive my speechifying. I am very tired and can not seem to find rest today.

June 21st

We received word today of Old Abe's proclamation to free the slaves. I do now believe, as others have said all along, that Abe is trying to ruin the South. We don't see many negroes around the battlefields, except those who help bury the dead. The Yanks who burned farmer's homes here in Virginia, gave the negroes the opportunity to run for freedom to the North. What can the negroes do but work for the farmer? That is all they know. What can they do on their own? Well, the captain said the other day for us to not get ourselves too tied up in all of these questions. He said just to fight for what we know to be right, and leave the rest in God's hands. We are sorely afflicted over the lack of mail that reaches us in camp. I would not place the blame on our kin, because we are aware of the state of deliveries due to the war and our frequent moves. But please, do not give up on reaching us, for it is all we soldiers live for.

June 23rd

Another day in camp with little to do. I was able to git some replacement socks from the dispensary. They are not new, but welcome just the same. Some of the men have been able to get pants and shirts from the hospital as well. These are clothes that were redeemed from the soldiers that was unlucky enough to die of their wounds. All parts of clothing and equipment must be used to help supply the soldiers in the field, as replacement articles are in very short supply. My regiment has been blessed to receive what amounts to one fair meal a day, for a month now. Many of our boys git much less to eat here. The lieutenant sent out a detail to forage in the area, but this area is picked pretty clean seems like. Some of the boys got mail today, and was troubled that their fields back home aren't planted yet. There are few men left to help the wives with planting while their husbands are gone to war. Of course this means that the soldiers families will have little to eat through the winter months, and nothing to sell for next seasons seed.

Our company has been under strength since the beginning of the month. We've lost about 70 men in this month alone. One of the camp guards caught a boy named Jack Higman trying to flee the camp to go home last night. The boy wasn't in our regiment, but we couldn't help but feel sorry for him. This morning he was brought before the whole camp assembled. They charged him with attempting to desert the army, striped him of his shirt, and tied him to the side of a wagon. He was sentenced to forty lashes on his back with the whip, but he collapsed after about twenty five lashes. His flesh was laid open to the bone. We was ordered to watch, or most of us would have missed the ordeal. The officers said that it should be a warning to the rest of us, that deserting carries this punishment. The word around camp is that the boy was just worried about his old Mama back home, and wanted to make that sure she is gitting by. The boy is sixteen years old. The doctor at the hospital tent said that he may die.

June 24th

There was some excitement in camp this morning when shots was heard to the west of camp. Our flank guards fired at some Yanks that was probably out foraging. This means that the Yankee army must be near. The word came down to see to our earthworks and muskets, and be ready to fight on short notice. Most of us spent the whole afternoon sitting behind our lines listening for signs of attack, but nothing happened.

June 25th

This morning we was roused early and sent quickly east to a small building called Ellerson's Mill. It was lightly treed and sloping slightly upward – not at all good ground, but we met the enemy there. The Yanks opened up with artillery which struck mostly to our companies right side. Our artillery was not in good position to return effective fire, but they poured in as much as they could and made a good show. As soon as the artillery stopped, we was ordered to advance toward the enemy. The Yanks began to fire at us even before we was in effective range. Our lieutenant yelled that they have plenty of ammunition to waste, so let them waste it, and we held our fire for a few more yards. On orders, our first line fired, then we moved up to do the same. The wind did not favor us, as it blew our musket smoke back into our faces and obscured our view of the enemy. We kept loading and firing, not able to clearly see the enemy, until we was ordered to retreat back about a hundred yards. As the smoke cleared, that same sight that we have seen before came into view. Hundreds of our boys lay before us on the ground. Some was crying for help, some was trying to crawl back to our lines, others was already dead. But we was ordered to advance again, and again we walked shoulder to shoulder, into their musket sights. Fire and load, fire and load. Again, I repeated the same course of action as before. The men on both sides of me were hit and killed. I kept up my action, hoping that by repeating the actions as I always had, I would again be spared. The noise and confusion was greater than I had ever seen. The wounded calling for help were around my feet, yet I could not attend to them. We advanced to a thin tree line, where we halted our advance. I took cover behind a tree and kept firing in the direction of the Yanks. I was running out of powder and shot when the firing ceased along our line. The lieutenant ordered us to take cover as we could and hold tight for further orders. As I looked past my tree, there was a Yank sitting next to the rock just a few yards away. He was badly wounded and could not move. We just stared at each other for a few moments, then he whispered, "Johnnie Reb. Can you hear me?" I answered back that I could. He said, "Do me a favor, son? Stick that bayonet of yours through me and save my misery. I'm done for anyway and I don't want to linger." Right then I remembered my trip to the hospital tent and that I wished for death rather than go there again. But I couldn't do it! I said that I was sorry to see him so distressed and wished that I could help. As we laid there staring at each other, a loud report sounded from off to my left, and the Yank slumped to his side. I felt kind of relieved for the Yank, but angry that a man would kill another when there was no reason to. I don't hate the Yanks. I just hate what they're doing. I think that maybe we're the same, the Yanks and us. We're both caught in the middle of following our officers orders and paying for the victory. This time, the Yank over there lost, and so far, I've won. One of the men said that he thinks of the Yanks as rabbits in his vegetable garden. As long as they keep getting in his garden, he is going to shoot them.

The Yanks called a truce so both sides could help the wounded and clear the dead off the battlefield. Some of our boys ran out and stole the packs off of some dead Yanks so they could get their rations and blankets. A few even took the shoes right off the bodies as they laid there. I wish I'd thought of that first, as my shoes are wearing thin as well. We had real coffee with our vittles tonight courtesy of the Yankee army.

When one of our sentries came off duty a while ago, he said that he had been having a conversation with the Yank sentry posted across the pasture. It seemed that the Yank was interested in where our sentry lived, and what kind of work he did back home. So they parleyed a while, and then the Yank told our man a story that he had heard about. It seemed that an old woman who lived up in north Virginia, had just cooked up the last bit of mush for her and her old husband when three Yankee soldiers rode up. Upon entering her house, they pushed her aside and commenced to eating all of her food. Just as they finished eating, the old lady came back into the kitchen, threw up her hands and cried, "Oh my, you have just eaten the poultice from my husband's sore leg." With that, the Yankees ran outside and immediately unswallowed. Well, the boys around the campfire thought that was a hoot! Of course, thinking back on our own supper tonight, I think that part about "unswallowing" seemed more a suggestion than a funny. Our sentry said that he and the Yank got pretty friendly as the evening progressed. They talked about their homes and loved ones, and what they expect to do after the fighting ends. This is a strange kind of war, I think. Here our boys are associating with the enemy in the evening, and then in the morning, they will be killing each other. I'm sure our old grandpappys didn't associate with the British army between battles, or our papas with the Indians in those fights either. I guess all the true hate of the enemy must be with the officers on both sides. It seems like we soldiers could talk out our differences. I hope all are well at home.

June 26th

There was more fighting to the west of our lines, but we wasn't involved today. We can see the Yanks across the pasture and it seems strange that we just sit here and watch each other. I'll write more tomorrow.

June 27th

This morning, near Gaine's Mill, the Yanks sent over some artillery shells that landed to the rear of our lines. Jeremy Lister, who was laying on the ground next to me after it started said, "I can't figure why the Yanks is shooting clear back there. There ain't nothing back there but the officers and killing them won't effect the war none." I had to laugh out loud. And you know, he may be right. I think I must be getting used to being shot at. There ain't no other reason to be laughing in an artillery shower.

I received your much cherished letter of May 25th tonight. I feel low over your news of the poor harvest expected in the fall. They say that it's been drier than usual here in Virginia this year also. I don't expect that my being home would change the situation any, but being so far away makes it harder to stomach. I was just thinking this morning how much our lives have changed since this awful war started. All the terrible trials started for us when Thomas passed. I really do miss him very much. I was just reflecting on when Thomas's dog, Bo died. Thomas was already thirteen by that time, but he carried on like it was the end of the world. I always felt that Thomas liked animals more than he did most folks. Thomas took such good care of that old dog because, I believe he thought that old dog took good care of him. Most days when we went to school up the old road toward Franklinton, that old dog would follow us right up to the door of the school house. When we came out, Bo would be right there waiting for Thomas. We had no idea where he was during the school's hours, but he was never late to go home. In the summers, when Thomas and me would go over to the river to swim, there was old Bo just a swimming right beside. I guess Thomas was right. Bo was a really good friend to him.

There's so many good Southern boys here, Mother Carruthers, and they're having to spend their lives too fast. So many are lost in each fight, that the grave diggers have to catch up to us at the next encampment due to the powerful lot of work that they have to do. The captain even commented on it the other day. He said, that we do "of course, expect the occasional empty chair, but no one expected the war to last more than a few months, and the cost to be so gravely high." Well, I'd better turn in as I have sentry duty at 2:00 AM.

June 30th

The battle continues, though without my participation. I have been confined for the last two days with the vexation of dysentery. The hospital is overcrowded as always. A young boy of sixteen was brought in last evening about seven o'clock with a musket ball wound in his heel. His foot was taken off by ten o'clock. It was badly done and with a dull knife. This morning the poor afflicted boy was in great pain and very sad. I determined to take his case upon myself and give him as much comfort as I can while I'm here, though I am to return to my company in the morning.

It is a blessing to many of the men here that some of the local ladies have come to offer their help in nursing the wounded. Three ladies came in just as daylight commenced and opened all the doors and tent flaps to clear the bad air. The wounded all began to grumble and shiver, but the ladies went on about their tasks. By the time that the sun was full up, there was ladies running to and fro filling water buckets, tearing down beds, piling blankets for the wash, and emptying the surgeon's buckets. Though their presence did cause quite a stir in the tents, I too was uplifted by their queenly forms and ministrations.

Many towns people came up from Richmond to see the battle going on. Some brought boxed lunches and spread their cloths under nearby trees to git front row seats of the proceedings. The captain complained that the visitors was clogging the roads and otherwise gitting in the way of the army's movements. A wounded sightseer was brought in to the hospital, supported on both sides by his friends. They said that the man was wounded by a stray bullet, and I could see that his hand was covered by blood. The doctor came a running to give aid to the man. After cleaning the man up, the doctor told him that he may lose the fingernail on his ring finger! He told the man, "Next time, stay out of the line of fire," and then abruptly left the room.

It is afternoon now, and it is mighty hot. There are so many foul smells mingling together around this hospital that one is liable to toss up his breakfast, if he is unlucky enough to have had any breakfast. A wounded corporal got a hold of some liquor last night and kicked up the devil a little while ago. They had to take off his left arm at the shoulder a few days ago, and this morning he broke away from the stewards and ran down the hill swearing like the blazes. The corporal is remembered as a respectable man, church folk, and used to mingle in good society down in New Orleans. But his buddies say that they can hardly stand him for the last six months. They say it is all the effects of his drinking to excess, when ever he can git the stuff. Anyway, three of the stewards jumped on him at the foot of the hill and brought him back to his blanket. He promptly dropped off to sleep with no more bicker.

We received some new troops this afternoon from Mississippi. Their lieutenant seems like an old granny. His troops seem to like him well enough, but I'd be surprised if he could give a firm command with both hands and a team of mules. We're hoping to git some Louisiana reinforcements in a few days time, they say. I hope that they are right, as our numbers lessen with each battle.

July 1st

I'm back on the line this morning even though I'm still feeling kind of puny. Gerome Tiller found some crackers and a hunk of dried beef in one of the Yankee haversacks that he stole yesterday, and was kind enough to share some with me this morning. I told him that if I survive the battle today, I'm going to look for some shoes that might fit before they clear the bodies off the field. I'd steal me some breeches too, but all the Yanks are wearing blue trousers, not proper for Southern men.

When the fighting started, the Yanks as is usual, gave us some artillery rounds to start. Then the soldiers rushed our lines. I should be dead right now, except for Jack Murey. When the fighting became hand to hand I was knocked down and a Yank saw his opportunity to run me through. Jack caught the Yank on the side of the head with his musket butt, then stuck him instead. I know that my time must be fast running out. I'm amazed that a man can go through a fight like this as many times as some of us have, and still be standing upright. The lieutenant just said that he believes that the Yanks are reforming in the gully so we have to get ready. I'll put my pen aside for now.

Well, the battle is over for the day looks like, and I got shot again! Actually, the bullet struck me in my ammunition pack. I'm not hurt, but listen to this! Gerome got shot in the canteen. When the water ran down his leg, he thought it was blood and fainted! I'm afraid that he's going to hear that story told around the cook fire for some time to come. But I think that for all the boasting in this army, no man can know how he will react when he is shot until it happens. I'm afraid that if I'm really shot, I will show that I am of no account, and will not take it like a man should. But tell Papa that I will continue to shoulder my musket as ordered, and I will try my best to make him proud to own me as his son.

July 3rd

One of the new recruits that arrived this morning from Richmond, brought with him some food to share with the company. This will prove that he is liked from the start. I can hardly believe what he said he paid for the stuff. He brought two turkeys that were $4.00 each, two geese that were $1.50 each, bacon at $.60 a pound, some lard at $1.00 a pound, and potatoes at $2.50 a bushel. He said that flour was $100.00 a barrel, so he could not get any of that. As you know, these are pretty high prices. The government does not furnish us with anything now but tough beef and corn meal. The supplies wagon pretends to issue us rations of rice, but $10.00 worth only lasts for about two meals. Last week, corn on the ear was issued instead of meal. I call this getting pretty low, don't you? After supper tonight, we all tried to remember when we had eaten so well, but could not. I guess it is a natural thing in war to talk about food since there is so little of it. A year or so ago, it would never have occurred to me to write you about our supper. I think, however, that we will all forever remember that this was our best meal of the year so far.

July 4th

Today is the birthday of the United States, and maybe the last one at that. Some of us was up as early as 2:00 AM, but not because we was excited about the day. Our stomachs are a little deranged from our supper last night. I think that our stomachs was surprised by some real food and could not remember what to do with it. Otis and Tom stayed up most of the night telling long yarns about bears and panthers, and such. These two are the damnedest liars you ever saw. The young boys who just joined us from Richmond, found a good night's sleep even tougher than usual after hearing those tall tales. But it won't be long before their childish fears turn into real nightmares.

July 5th

My health is poorly this morning since I am again afflicted with dysentery and severe pains in my stomach and bowels. I have no fever obvious, yet I feel very weak. I again stopped by the hospital to get some medicine, but the doctor could not be sure of the cause of my affliction. I swear that there is a wonderous amount of ignorance in the medical practices. It seems that most of them will give a large dose of calomel to the patient no matter what his ailment may be. Then comes dose after dose of quinine and other strong medicines until they either kill the patient or ruin his constitution for life. The doctor gave me a couple of pills made of Blue Mass, which he said would clean me out. I did not take them since my problem is just the opposite.

We had a nice summer storm this afternoon and so just stayed in our tents, as my affliction allowed. One of the boys offered to lend me a book that he carried with him, but as you know, I'm not much for book reading.

The word in camp is that the enemy has retreated from our location (Mechanicsville) back to the north. This news, if we can trust it, has truly lifted the boys' spirits here in camp.

July 7th

I was feeling much better this morning and our company was sent to the east of camp to help build a corduroy road. That is what they call a road that is paved with small tree trunks laid across the cleared dirt. It is a good road to move wagons over as they will not bog down in ruts or mud. For anyone riding in the wagons though, it will shake their insides loose for sure. But we built a dandy one. It was good to get a day of hard labor to work out the gloom of camp life. By the by, tell Papa that I got a pair of breeches from the hospital while I was there. Tonight for supper, we had a rare treat. They could not git coffee, so they used parched corn. Oh, the lovely soldier's life.

July 8th

Well, I finally made it to Richmond! This morning, those of us that felt so disposed, were allowed to hike over to town. Richmond is the biggest city you can imagine! Geroam and I took it upon ourselves to see as much of the city as time allows. We're resting right now at the corner of Governor and Carey Streets, near the railroad tracks. There are many two and three story buildings and bigger. We saw the Libby and Son Company where Uncle Horace used to get his chewing tobacco, and Haxall's Flour Mill, the biggest building I ever seen. Earlier we saw the Washington Monument that honor's the first president. It is really beautiful. It must be more than 50 feet high, made of stone and bronze, with thirteen stars around the top under the statue. We saw the wharf section on the James River where all the ships are tied up. You would not believe the number of great ships that are coming and going here abouts. From Canal Basin we could see the great Customs House, and not far away, the State Capitol building that they say was designed by Thomas Jefferson. There are several great universities and seminaries here also. There are shops that sell everything imaginable, but many were closed up due to the fighting nearby. We could see St. John's Church from a fair distance. It was built in 1741, one of the very oldest buildings in the city they say. It must be the most beautiful church in the world. We stepped inside for a moment and the insides are even more beautiful that the outsides. It is the most wonderous sight I ever seen.

There are many row houses and great houses in the city also. Pardon my speaking plain, but there are also very many houses where the ladies are eager to "relieve the stresses of men's war duties," as Geroam was quick to point out. But everywhere we went, the townspeople were quick to thank us for saving them from the Yankee hordes, as they called them. I told Geroam that I thought the real heroes was the good boys that they could no longer thank. He agreed with me. We was told that there are about 20,000 men that was killed or wounded in the last two weeks in the fighting that we was in. Lord, what a mess this country is in. Well, Geroam and I have to start back to camp, so I'll close for now.

July 9th

On our way back to camp yesterday, Geroam and I saw a man who had gotten his wagon stuck off the road in some mud. His two mules looked like they were done in from their in vain efforts at pulling him out. But even with our help, the old man could not get the wagon to move. Then he saw two negroes coming up the road and yelled at them to lend a hand. At first they tried to ignore the old man, but then he raised his musket at them and said that he would drop one of them right where they was standing if they both did not come and help. Very reluctantly they came and with our help was able to shove the old man's wagon back onto the road. Probably being frightened gave the negroes the strength to make the difference. But we had no further trouble with them.

This afternoon, the whole division was called out to see a man shot for desertion. They said that they was going to shoot him, instead of whip him, because he ran during the battle. The poor boy had to dig his own grave, then they sat him on the end of his coffin at the edge of the hole. A detachment of six guards was formed, one of them having a blank cartridge in his rifle. On the order, they all fired and it was done. I heard that there was other men executed in the other camps too. Some men just don't have it in them to kill another man. There was six Yanks caught by our sentries trying to sneak away from their army. We will probably shoot them too. Tomorrow we are to have an Inspection, so we are busy cleaning our muskets, and such.

July 11th

A couple of the boys and me went out yesterday to cut some wood for our cook fires. The ax was as dull as an old hoe, but I took my turn as usual. Somehow, I guess I was mind wandering, anyhow the ax slipped and I put a dandy gash in my left foot. I had to go back to the surgeon and have seven stitches in it. It made the sweat roll off me in big drops while he sewed it up. I told him that he is a very rough tailor because it was all I could do to hold in the pain he caused. My foot is now swollen and very sore. The doc said that I'd have to stay off of it for a week or so. Now doesn't that about burn your vittles! We finally get some relief from this war, and I have to stay down and nurse my foot. Some of the boys are going back to Richmond tomorrow, but I will be staying right here on my behind, sweating with the heat and swatting mosquitoes. Maybe I can go next week, war permitting.

The weather has been tolerably cool during the night, but the days have been increasingly hot and humid. It reminds me of home. I haven't had the pleasure of receiving your good letters for weeks. I pray that all is well with you and my Papa, and that the delay is because the old mail horse died, or something the like. I have not heard any gun fire for a couple of days, not even our own out foraging. This morning there was no food for breakfast, only some chicory coffee and a small piece of hardtack. I believe the food is the worst part of war, excepting the killing. More of our boys will likely perish this month from lack of food, and of course sickness, rather than from being shot by the enemy. Most of the diseases are passed by the men who chase after bad women, get the disease, then take the measles or some other on top of it. I believe that I can live as healthy here as at home if I don't weaken.

The news today from Richmond is good. It seems that we have the Yanks on the run everywhere in the South. Maybe it is true that the war will be over soon. I think often about coming home to Papa's farm and returning to good clean work, rather than war work. I know things won't be the same after the war, though. I must tell you, though it may bring you some pain, that I think of Thomas every day and night. I still have a hard time believing that he is gone forever. I feel like when I git home that Thomas will come a'running through our gate to greet me as he always has. I was recollecting how Thomas fell out of ole "spooky tree" when he was twelve, and broke his arm. If I'm recollecting true, Thomas told you that he broke it wrestling your hog back into the pen. He knew you'd be mad if you knew because you had told him to stay out of that tree. Anyway, afterward he just sat there on the ground and cried as though the world had ended. Then his old dog, Bo, came a'running and just about licked Thomas's face off. Then Thomas was fine. So he and I when over to Papa's farm to have him straighten out Thomas's arm and tie it up. Then he made up the hog story to save himself a swatting. He was a funny boy, and the best friend that I will ever have.

July 12th

My foot is still swollen and powerful sore. Please take heed, and tell Pa also, that from the reports here in camp, if the Yanks come through, they will steal everything and starve you out. We were told that the Yanks we caught a running from their own lines said that they have been ordered to burn all the barns, etc., and steal all the food, and make the people in the South suffer as much as possible. One of our detachments up north, we are told, came upon a burning house with an old man and three girls. The old man had tears on his face when he said that the Yanks responsible even took his dead wife's favorite mule. Well, our boys caught the Yanks trying to burn another house, and taught them what for. They got the Yanks' horses and the old man's mule and returned it to him. It just made our blood boil to hear of such treatment. We hear stories every day about all the terrible things that the Yanks are doing to our people, especially to the helpless farmers and their families. It is difficult to believe all that we hear, and I try to believe that they are just soldier's stories. How can the Northerners be so cruel to us?

July 14th

With much pleasure I received your letter of May 20 today. I must thank you again for keeping Papa informed with my letters. Yours are the only letters I git, as you and Papa are the only ones I know, and only you can write. My foot is still keeping me down, and too swollen to get my shoe on. But the doc says that I will survive. The stores wagon was by this morning and gave each man about 3 inches of bar soap. It is funny to see a dozen men down at the creek washing their shirts and singing up a storm. I have not had a bath in over two weeks and the doc now says that I must keep my injured foot dry, so I don't know what I can do. In a few days I'll drag myself down to the creek and give myself a hand dousing.

The boys brought some things back from their last trip to Richmond, mostly liquor. They said that the food was scarce and expensive. The only thing in plentiful supply was the women. Geroam says that the townspeople are hoarding most things in the belief that the Yanks are going to come back to Richmond. I'll write more as I can.

July 24th

I am sorry that I have not written for about ten days. My foot is better, and I am pleased to be up and about some now. We have had afternoon rains for the last several days and a couple of them about washed out the camp. It is difficult to stay dry in these little tents. We have not lifted our muskets against the enemy in nearly a month. We are all completely bored and without much hope of our situation changing in the near future. Some of the boys was able to get away from camp on foraging marches. I am still unable to keep up the march due to my foot, and so I am bound to the area between our tent and the hospital.

Geroam and some of the boys was detailed to hike over to the Virginia Central Railroad depot and pick up some supplies for the camp. Two of the boys were betting on whether there was real coffee or not with the supplies. As it turned out, there was little of any rations in the shipment. He said there was six barrels of rancid salted pork, a few bags of rice, beans, and as ever, hardtack. There is still no mention of replacement shoes, breeches, or shirts. I wager that I will have to pay another visit to the hospital to get some new clothes.

My enlistment is up on the 26th, but the officers expect me to re-enlist. It is hard to believe that I have been in this army for a whole year. I heard one of the new boys singing a song that Thomas and I used to sing from our Fifth Reader in school. The old wood school house that we went to up in Franklinton, came to mind. I thought about my old schoolmates, my boyhood companions, many of them now scattered and far away in the service of their country, some, like Thomas, who have already given up their lives. It made me pine to be home again. I decided to not re-enlist, but to go home where I can help Papa with the farm. I know that he has had a time of it since I went off to fight. I have given a year to my country, now I just want to get as far away from this war as I can. I want some real homemade cooking, a night of restful sleep when I don't have to keep one ear open for enemy attacks. I want to come back home to the plains of Washington Parish, Louisiana, where I growed up.

But I can not go home. I can't go home as long as there are invaders in our land. I can not abandon the field of battle after so many of my classmates and countrymen have given their lives and futures to the honor of the South. We soldiers complain about our discomforts and trials, about our lack of food and clothing, about disease, and the many miles most of us have marched. But each time we dig a grave, or pass a burial place, we must be thankful to be called upon in this terrible time to display our faithfulness to our home and loved ones. I know Papa will understand that I must stay until the fighting is done. I have to re-enlist, or let my country down. Papa, I could not live with myself if I didn't stay for those boys who will never go home.

July 26th

Yesterday I re-enlisted. Today the 1st, 2nd, 10th, 15th, and our 9th Regiments were reformed into the 2nd Louisiana Brigade from the leftovers of the 1st Louisiana, so write me there. Despite our victories, our numbers still lessen. A courier from President Davis arrived in camp last night. After his confab with the officers, he sat with us around the cook fire. He had a lot of information about the war to tell us. But I must tell you of a new song that he taught us. General Albert Pike made up the words that are to be sung to the tune of "Dixie." I will relate his words to the "new Dixie" as best I can.

Southrons, hear your country call you!
Up lest worse than death befall you!
To arms! To arms! To arms, in Dixie!
Lo, all the beacon fires are lighted,
Let all hearts be now united!
To arms! To arms! To arms, in Dixie!

Advance the flag of Dixie!
Hurrah, Hurrah!
For Dixie's land we take our stand
and live or die for Dixie!
To arms! To arms!
And conquer peace for Dixie!
To arms! To arms!
And conquer peace for Dixie!

Hear the Northern thunders mutter!
Northern flags in South winds flutter!
Send them back your fierce defiance!
Stamp upon the cursed alliance!
 To arms, etc.

Fear no danger! Shun no labor!
Lift up rifle, pike, and saber!
Shoulder pressing close to shoulder!
Let the odds make each heart bolder!
 To arms, etc.

How the South's great heart rejoices
At your cannon's ringing voices!
For faith betrayed, and pledges broken,
Wrong inflicted, insults spoken,
 To arms, etc.

Strong as lions, swift as eagles,
Back to their kennels hunt these beagles!
Cut the unequal bonds asunder!
Let them hence each other plunder!
 To arms, etc.

Swear upon you country's altar,
Never to submit or falter,
Till the spoilers are defeated,
Till the Lord's work is completed!
 To arms, etc.

I am sure that these swell words will help rally our boys to victory! And I hope victory comes soon. Please write often, news from home is all we boys have.

July 29th

I am finally able to join the boys on a hike to Richmond. My foot is much better and I am ever more ready to git out of camp for the day. Soon after we arrived in Richmond, we saw the strangest thing. A town photographer was showing from his wagon, a picture of a large balloon with a man standing in a basket underneath it. The balloon floated high over a field within view of our Capital. He said that he took the picture when the Yanks was a few miles away, back at the beginning of the month. The man in the basket is named Thaddeus Lowe and he invented the contraption. The Yanks was using the balloon to take a man high up in the air to see what we was doing from a long distance away. Then the man would sent messages down to the troops on the ground by telegraph and they would attack us by the information sent down. The photographer said that it is one of the new, modern weapons of war that is in use against us. It seems to me that a man could git a fine view from up there, but his balloon is an awful big target as well. I bet that there is no Southern rifleman who could not hit a target of that size even at a distance. A couple of the boys and I had a picture taken of us to be sent home. So tell Papa that it will be arriving soon. In the news today, we read of fighting near Owensville, Kentucky, and near Chattanooga, Tennessee. You will recollect that we went through Chattanooga on the cars last year on our way to Manassas Junction. Well, thanks to news reporters in the area, Richmond gits the New York Times newspaper only about a day or two after press.

It is nice that the Times allows that the South should be kept so up to date on the movements of the Yanks. One of the papers from a week or two ago had a write up about the fighting that took place at Malvern Hill earlier this month. It describes how some Yank Major-General Fitz-John Porter used his artillery to such advantage that he "savaged the Confederate drive up Malvern Hill." Lord, they sure can make a defeat sound like a victory! Old Abe Lincoln called General McClellan's campaign a "half defeat." The boys and I can not figure out what that particular Northern military talk means, since we chased all the Yanks clear out of Virginia! We are wondering which half of their defeat that they consider the victory.

According to the papers, at their fourth of July celebration the enemy recognized the anniversary with "forbidden sport" and rest, the paper says. The General reported that all was quiet along their lines, except for a sharp demonstration of the Confederates on the James River which killed or wounded some twenty of their men. We boys resolved that the next time we see the Yanks, we will give them some more restful days!

The boys wanted to go down to the docks and see the gunboats that was there, so we did. Then we split up, as the other boys wanted to try their luck at tempting disease. I walked back into town to see the sights of the city from Oregon Hill, then headed back to camp. The boys got back to camp late, and the Lieutenant chided them for it. They will now be staying in camp for a few days. The light is fading so I will have to close. Give my love to all. I'll write again soon.

August 7th

We received word of fighting against the Yanks this morning at Culpepper Court House and near Madison Court House up by Manassas Junction. We then got orders to break camp and prepare to move north to engage the enemy. We was on the cars by late afternoon. There is much complaining about the way this army sits around for weeks doing nothing, then has to move 70 or 80 miles and prepare to fight on a few hours notice. The complaints a few days ago was that we was wasting away instead of taking part in the fighting. I do believe that soldiers will find something to complain about no matter what. At least we had time to choke down some rice and dried fruit before we loaded the cars.

August 8th

The train stopped at Fredericksburg this morning before light. We commenced to unloading the cars and organizing our regiment on a nearby hill overlooking the city. Once done, we had time to relax and take a look at the town. From the hill, Fredericksburg is another big city like Richmond. There are only three or four church steeples sticking up from the rows of wooden houses and shops. From here it does not look as dirty as Richmond is, though we are a half mile distant from the city. The orders have come to form up for the march, so I have to put my pen aside for now.

August 9th

Yesterday's march north took us well into the night. When we finally stopped to rest in a clearing, we did not put up our tents or make camp. After about four hours time to sleep we was on the march again. We crossed the Rapid River, and arriving at Southwest Mountain, commenced to engaging the enemy skirmishers in light action. We received no casualties in our section, and the area is quiet at the moment. I'll put your letter aside for now in favor of sleep. My love to all.

August 10th

I slept late this morning as there is no fighting in our area. A war correspondent came by this morning and commenced to telling us of his talks with the prisoners from yesterday's battle. One of the wounded that he talked to was a Yankee Captain by the name of O'Brien from the 3rd Wisconsin Regiment. The Captain told the reporter that a Rebel surgeon came to him on the field and told him that he had no chance of living, gave him some water to drink, and left him on the field. Later, some Rebel soldiers came up and took his watch, cut out his pocket containing $260, and left him to die there. He was finally brought off the field under a flag of truce, but would not survive the night. The reporter said that he got the statement from the dying man's lips.

The view of the battlefield was a sight I'll never forget. For nearly a mile the dead lay scattered or in heaps, many torn, or cut apart by the shells, some without heads. The bodies of our courageous countrymen laid right up to the enemy's line of artillery. Some of our Louisiana boys are missing this afternoon. We got reinforcements from Richmond today, but the main problem is food. No one in our company has eaten a thing since last night, and our strength is rapidly leaving us. Many of the men openly pray for God to send food since Jeff Davis won't. But it is not his fault. Even the foragers come back night after night with not one cow, or even a possum, for the army to eat. Shall we eat the enemy's dead horses right off the battlefield, or our own mules? (The mule as a tasty meal is a downright failure, you have my oath on it!)

Word comes today of General Breckenridge's attack on the Yanks at Baton Rouge on the 5th. All in camp are grieved that our boys were pushed back from the city. At least one of the Yankee Generals was killed. I am concerned from your letter telling of highjackers in your area. There has been some Yankee raiders here in Virginia too that rob and burn the houses, and debase our Southern women. Tell Papa to keep his musket loaded and close by. Mother Carruthers, tell your negro man not to run but to protect you if any of these rabble come your way.

August 11th

This morning our company moved the camp from the grounds of the Piedmont School near Crittenden Lane over to Mitchell's Station at the foot of Southwest Mountain. I'm not sure why we don't just fight right here. The Yanks are right on our tails with every move we make. The boys want to turn on them and give them the what for. From time to time, the Yank snipers take a shot at our lines but we won't respond unless they come out into the open. Our officers just keep saying to keep our heads down and wait for orders.

There is a lot of wounded and dead being moved from earlier battles to the rear today. Most of the boys are dressed just in rags, and bare foot. The older men are still wearing the coats that they brought with them a year ago. I don't have to tell you what a year of tramping through the brush in winter snow and summer heat can do to a body's clothes. The enemy artillery fire has been a fairly common sound for the last few days. It has not been directed into our area so far, but I can hear it mostly all day long. I am happy to receive your too short letter today.

August 13th

I am waiting for orders to march again this morning. General Lee has ordered us to fall back to Gordonsville, and dig in for battle. The boys and me have broken camp and are ready to move. There has been some light fighting since last night all around our area. The boys are really ready to get into this scrap.

Our regiment has set up its lines outside of Gordonsville. The officers believe that we will make contact with the enemy later this afternoon. The Yank scouts show up from time to time just to make sure that we are still here, I think. I am going to stop writing now and make ready for the fight.

August 15th

Dear Mrs. Carruthers, my name is Geroam Tiller. I am part of the same Regiment as Ford is. He asked me to write to you and tell you of the sad fact that Ford was wounded in battle the afternoon of the 13th. He was shot in the left arm just above the elbow and the doctor had to remove his arm. He was also shot in the side, but not badly. Ford is in grievous misery over his luck, but the doctor expects that he will live. In a few days, Ford will be able to write you hisself. I must admit to you my own misery about Ford, as I will no longer have such a good friend to fight beside me. Please forgive my boldness in writing to you, but Ford talks of his family so much that I believe that I fairly know you all. My regards, Geroam.

August 17th

I have been moved to the hospital near Richmond, and now feel strong enough to send my regards. Please do not worry about me, or let Papa worry either, the war is over for me. The doctors tell me that I will be on my way home before too many days. My side wound just needed a few more stitches from our medical tailor and it will be fine. Tell Papa that I am sorry that I got shot and lost my arm. I know that I will be more a burden to him than help from now on, and Papa works so hard already. But tell him that I will make it up to him some how.

I have not yet gotten over the surgeon's work. When he sawed my arm off, he gave me a dirty rag to bite down on, and two other men held me down. It seemed to take forever, sawing away like he did. I was afraid that I would pass out, or start yelling like some of the other men did before me. The doc said that I did real good, though. I don't think that I would have made you shameful of me, Papa. Today the pain is lessened to the point that I can take some time to write you and let you know that I will be fine. I will write again soon with some idea of when you can expect to see me again. My love and regards to all.

August 18th

I would surely cherish receiving a kind letter from you today. I am in deep misery over my condition. We received word today that General Winder was killed the same day that I got shot. Several other generals and high officers were killed or captured too. I fear that things are not going well for our cause. I will be taken to the hospital at Petersburg with the rest of the useless soldiers tomorrow and I will see what kind of arrangements I can make to come home. I regret to tell you that most of my personal things, including my musket, were lost when I was carried from the battlefield. I am sorry for the loss. I am not sure how long I remained on the field after I was shot, but the action began about four o'clock in the afternoon and it was after dark when I reached the surgeon's tent, and close to midnight before the surgeon had his way with me. Papa paid twelve dollars for my musket when I was ten years old, and now it is gone. I suppose that a one-armed man could not fairly shoot a musket anyway.

I don't know how much longer that I can stand to be in this hospital. The pain and agony of the wounded here never stops. The cries for help, for hunger, and for home, are constant day and night, with little relief from the doctors. There are so many boys, no older than fourteen years, that are brought here with grievous wounds. Yet, many of them take great pride in their wounds so honorably received. The town ladies that come each morning to help with the sick seem to spend as much time as they can with the younger boys. They treat the boys like their very own. Then, when one dies of his wounds, it is like they have lost their own son. The ladies' kind aid is treasured, yet, this is still the saddest place in the world. I could never have believed that my world could change so much in the short time of one year.

August 21st

I hope all are well at home. The doctor here at the Petersburg Hospital says that it will be a few more weeks before I can go home. They say that I can not leave until I am nearly well. My wounds are healing just fine I think, but the doctors will make up their own minds. I arrived here by the cars yesterday, and did get a look at the city from the depot. Not too far from the depot is the Castle Thunder Prison for the Yanks that have been captured. I could see it from the tracks. There is a place called Fort Sedgwick that is supposed to be nearby, but I did not see it. I've heard since then that some of the troops call it "Fort Hell" because the whole fort is made from big baskets woven from branches and then filled with sand. There are no walls or real protection for the troops, just rows of basket-walls. Later, they took us in carts to the Hospital nearby, which is in a beautiful spot. There are a lot of trees for shade and good clean water. There are wooden buildings here, besides the tents, which will keep us dry during storms, and there are many ladies that come from town to help out with the wounded. This morning I met Corporal Miller Askins who I will be sharing a small tent with. He was wounded three days before I was, at Culpepper Court House. I believe that his wounds are more grievous than mine, for he has lost both of his legs. I should try to not git low over the loss of my arm. There are many, many more soldiers with much more to be saddened about. I have learned how to dress and take care of myself with one hand, but I will have to work out some new way to lace-up my shoes. I aim to be able to take care of myself by the time I git home.

The New York Times of August 15th is being passed among the wounded at the hospital. There is an account which they got from the Richmond Dispatch, in which they give the Southern side of the battles, which they call the battles of Cedar Mountain. It says that we captured some thirty commissioned officers in the battles. There is also a nice article on General Jackson. The fighting goes on in the area of Manassas where it all began for our regiment. There is nothing more new with me, I will write again soon.

August 28th

I am feeling tolerable and progressing well the doctors say. I was sorry to hear that old Uncle Cletus passed away. I think it is a good idea for Papa to bury him on the hill near Mama. It is right for the dead to spend their eternity with relatives near by. All the soldiers that are dying in this war are just buried near where they fell, except for most of the high officers. At least I know that I won't be buried in a foreign land now. It would be unthinkable to be buried in the North, should General Lee ever decide to take this war to them. I believe that the Yanks do not know how much Southern men love their country. I am sure that this solid love, and God's might of course, is what will lead us surely to victory.

There are more and more casualties coming in from the fighting up near Manassas. They say that the numbers killed are very high too. I feel like I should be up there in the fight, not just sitting around here for weeks. If they would give me a pistol, I could still fight. I don't know how I will feel, me going home with the fighting still going on.

August 29th

Dear beloved family, when I arose from my tent this morning I was met with the most sickening sight of my life. As far as I could see, the grounds were covered with wounded soldiers that were brought in during the night. The hospital building was full, the tents were crowded, everywhere outside laid our boys with hardly room to walk between them. In every direction that I looked, every time I opened my eyes, all I could see was the red of blood. There was more red than the brown of the ground, or the green of the trees. The orderlies and surgeons were all covered with blood. Everywhere I looked was suffering and death. Then an orderly pushed a cart right by me that was filled to the top with the work of the surgeons. Arms and legs and pieces of bodies from the beloved sons of our land were being taken to the outside to be dumped into shallow trenches. Suddenly, I retched upon the ground right in front of my tent. I was distressed to make such a show of myself in front of everyone, but when I could look up, I saw that no one even noticed me. Oh Lord, please make this fighting stop! We are all dying! Since that time, I have stayed in my tent with Miller. I am sure that they will soon need our tent for the wounded, and we will gladly move to other quarters. I must beg your pardon for the coarseness of my letter. It is not my wish that you should become distressed by what I have written. But I feel that I must say how I feel to someone or become demented by its vision. Please forgive me.

September 1st

I can leave for home tomorrow! I will ride a supply train west to the junction of the Jackson Railroad at Jackson, Mississippi. I am not sure what my plans will be from there, but by then, I will be smelling-distance from home! If I can, I will take the Jackson train back to Camp Moore, visit Thomas, and then walk home from there.

Word reached us at the hospital tonight, that men of the 2nd Louisiana Regiment ran out of ammunition at Manassas on the 30th and threw rocks at the Yanks until new ammunition was brought up to the line. I guess the old boys can still handle the Yanks! We also heard of the fighting that's been going on in Baton Rouge and New Orleans in past days. Now they say that there is fighting in Lafourche Parish too. It sounds like that by the time I git home the fighting will be right at our front door step. Please take care until I git home, and tell Papa too.

September 6th

I arrived at Camp Moore today on the cars. There were only about thirty soldiers here. The soldiers say that General Thompson sent some prisoners here from Ponchatoula in August. But there has been no training going on here since July. I will spend the night here, then set out for home in the morning.

I went back to the grave yard right away to visit Thomas. I just could not stay away. I had no trouble finding his grave even though the markers are all thrown about. I sat down on the ground beside him and thought about all the times we had growing up. I was thankful that he did not have to see all the things that I had to see. Maybe the good Lord took him before our fighting began because He knew that Thomas would have suffered grievously from the hardship and terror.

As I sit here, writing my last war letter to you, I decided, with your permission of course, to petition the army to have Thomas removed from the cemetery so that I can bring him back home to rest. Most of the boys buried here at Camp Moore are young, as Thomas was. Most of them here, like Thomas, died from disease, not battle. Most of them were unmourned, their names and faces forgotten except to God. Thomas and me went to war together and we will come home together. We are both sons of our beloved South. And when my time comes to leave this earth, I will rest beside Thomas on the hill between our farms, under old "spooky tree."

Glossary of Terms

"Ante up"   a term used among soldiers of the period meaning to "put up one's share." In terms of battle, a reference to putting one's life on the line as others are doing.

Breeches   also called knee breeches, Knee-length trousers commonly worn by men and boys of the 17th, 18th, and 19th, centuries.

Calomel   a white, tasteless powder used chiefly as a fungicide and a purgative.

"Cars"   a period term used chiefly in reference to railroad cars, or trains in general.

Comeuppance   a slang term referring to someone

who got his just reward, usually unpleasant, what a person has coming to him.

Commissary   a store (army) that supplies food and equipment for purchase.

Daguerreotype   a photographic process invented in 1839 by L.J.M. Daguerre, in which a picture is made by exposing light to a silver surface (usually tin) sensitized with iodine and developed by exposure to mercury vapor. An early popular photograph.

Dog-trot cabin   a slang term (Southern) meaning a small cabin of loose construction, built in a leisurely manner, like the gentle trot of a dog, not a serious construction.

Dysentery   a period term for diarrhea, marked by inflammation and ulceration of the lower bowels, causes bleeding and sometimes even death.

Fancy ladies   a period term assuming the immorality of a woman by her habit of outlandish dress. A prostitute or a mistress.

"Fever"   a general period term for any of a

group of diseases in which high fever is a prominent symptom. Examples are yellow fever, malaria, scarlet fever, and measles.

Haversack   a soldier's bag for carrying food, extra clothes, or personal items.

Quartermaster   the army officer charged with providing quarters, clothing, transportation, etc., for a body of troops.

Quinine   a white, bitter, alkaloid obtained from cinchona bark, used in medicine chiefly in the treatment of malaria, a group of diseases causing chills, fever, and hallucinations, is reoccurring, and caused by parasitic protozoans introduced to the human bloodstream by mosquitoes.

"Levee rats"   a period term referring to low-life men associated with the rivers or docks.

Bibliography

Casey, Powell A. *The Story of Camp Moore and Life at Camp Moore Among the Volunteers.* United States: FPHC Inc., Bourque Printing, 1985.

Patrick, Robert. *Reluctant Rebel – The Secret Diary of Robert Patrick – 1861-1865.* Baton Rouge: Louisiana State University Press.

Bergeron, Jr., Arthur W. *Guide to Louisiana Confederate Units – 1861-1865.* Baton Rouge: Louisiana State University Press, 1996.

Eisenschiml, O. and R. Newman. *The Civil War: An American Iliad.* New York: Konecky and Konecky, 1956.

Bradford, Ned. *Battles and Leaders of the Civil War.* New York: Fairfax Press, 1988.

Chisolm, Daniel. *Civil War Notebook.* New York: Orion Books, 1989.

"Civil War letters to Albert from Charles." Archival Letters, 1861. Baton Rouge: Louisiana State University – Hill Memorial Library.

Jennings, Virginia L. *The Plains and the People.* Baton Rouge: Land and Land Printers, 1989.

Sanders, Mary E. *Diary in Gray – Letters and Diary of Jared Young Sanders.* Camp Moore Archives, Kenwood, Louisiana.

Brumgardt, John R. *Civil War Nurse – Diary and Letters of Hannah Ropes.* Knoxville: University of Tennessee Press, 1980.

McHenry, Howard. *Recollections of a Maryland Confederate Soldier and Staff Officer.* Ohio: Morningside Bookshop, 1975.

"Richmond". *Microsoft Encarta Encyclopedia.* New York: Funk and Wagnalls, 1993-95.

Albaugh/Simmons. *Confederate Arms.* New York: Bonanza Books, 1957.

Russell, Andrew J. *Russell's Civil War Photographs.* New York: Dover Publications, 1982.

The New York Times Book of the Civil War. Ed. Arleen Keylin and Douglas Bowen. New York: Arno Press, 1980.

Commanger, Henry S. *The Civil War Almanac.* New York: Facts On File Inc., 1982.

Wiley, Bell Irvin. *The Life of Johnny Reb.* Baton Rouge: Louisiana State University Press, 1990.

Soldiering – Diary of R. C. Bull. Ed. K. Jack Bawr. New York: Berkley Books, 1988.

Hammond, M. *Such is a Soldiers Life – Letters of George A. Hammond, USA.* Tucson: Admiral Press, 1994.

Mitchell, Patricia B. *Confederate Camp Cooking.* Virginia: Sims/Mitchell House, 1992.

"Letters of John A. Harris." Louisiana State Special Collections. Baton Rouge: Louisiana State University.

Lossing, Benson J. *Matthew Brady's Illustrated History of the Civil War.* New York: Fairfax Press.

Bettman, Otto L. *The Good Old Days – They Were Terrible.* New York: Random House, 1974.

Hard Marching Everyday – Civil War Letters of Wilbur Fisk. Ed. Emil & Ruth Rosenblatt. Kansas City: University Press of Kansas, 1992.

Katcher, Philip. *The Civil War Source Book.* New York: Facts on File Inc., 1995.

Bell/South Advertising and Publishing. Washington Parish, Louisiana. 1995.